THANKS TO JOSEFINA

JOSEFINA · 1824

BY VALERIE TRIPP

ILLUSTRATIONS JEAN-PAUL TIBBLES

VIGNETTES RENÉE GRAEF, SUSAN MCALILEY

THE AMERICAN GIRLS COLLECTION®

Published by Pleasant Company Publications

Visit our Web site at **americangirl.com**

Printed in Singapore.
03 04 05 06 07 08 09 10 TWP 10 9 8 7 6 5 4 3 2

Library of Congress Cataloging-in-Publication Data

Tripp, Valerie, 1951–
Thanks to Josefina / by Valerie Tripp ;
illustrations, Jean-Paul Tibbles ; vignettes, Renée Graef, Susan McAliley.
p. cm. — (The American girls collection)
Summary: In 1824 New Mexico, Josefina and her sisters argue as they weave, until
Josefina thinks of a way to make their work more fun. Includes historical notes on
blanket weaving in New Mexico in 1824 and instructions for dyeing a T-shirt.
ISBN 1-58485-698-X
[1. Weaving—Fiction. 2. Sisters—Fiction. 3. Mexican Americans—Fiction.
4. New Mexico—History—To 1848—Fiction.]
I. Tibbles, Jean-Paul, ill. II. Graef, Renée, ill.
III. McAliley, Susan. IV. Title. V. Series.
PZ7.T7363 Th 2003
[Fic]—dc21   2002029666

The
AMERICAN GIRLS
COLLECTION®

OTHER AMERICAN GIRLS
SHORT STORIES:

PICTURE CREDITS

The following individuals and organizations have generously given permission to reprint illustrations contained in "Looking Back": p. 32—Museum of International Folk Art, Santa Fe, NM; p. 33—Sheep, photo by Nancy Hunter Warren from *Villages of Hispanic New Mexico,* copyright 1987 by Nancy Hunter Warren, School of American Research, Santa Fe; Carding brushes, courtesy Kathy Borkowski; p. 34—Courtesy Galen R. Frysinger; p. 35—Blanket, School of American Research, cat. #IAF.T25; Basket, School of American Research, cat. #IAF.B248; p. 38—Museum of International Folk Art, Santa Fe, NM; p. 39—From *The Saltillo Sarape,* Santa Barbara Museum of Art; p. 40—Wisconsin Historical Society; p. 41—© Wolfgang Kaehler/CORBIS; p. 42—Photography by Jamie Young.

TABLE OF CONTENTS

PAPÁ
*Josefina's father, who
guides his family
and his rancho with
quiet strength.*

ANA
*Josefina's oldest sister,
who is married and has
two little boys.*

JOSEFINA
*A nine-year-old girl
whose heart and
hopes are as big as
the New Mexico sky.*

FRANCISCA
*Josefina's fifteen-year-old
sister, who is headstrong
and impatient.*

CLARA
*Josefina's practical,
sensible sister, who is
twelve years old.*

TÍA DOLORES
*Josefina's aunt, who
has lived far away in
Mexico City for ten years.*

TERESITA
*Tía Dolores's servant,
an excellent weaver.*

Josefina and her family speak Spanish, so you'll see some Spanish words in this book. If you can't tell what a word means from reading the story or looking at the illustrations, you can turn to the "Glossary of Spanish Words" on page 48. It will tell you what the word means and how to pronounce it.

Remember that in Spanish, "j" is pronounced like "h." That means Josefina's name is pronounced "ho-seh-FEE-nah."

THANKS TO JOSEFINA

On a bright, blue-sky day in late October, Josefina Montoya and her sisters were working in the weaving room. Ana, the eldest, was weaving at one of the large looms. She hummed as she worked, and the peaceful *thump, thump* of the foot pedals made a rhythm as gentle as breathing. Francisca was spinning wool into yarn, and Clara was carding wool to get the tangles out. Josefina was half-sitting, half-kneeling in

1

front of a smaller hanging
loom. Slowly and carefully,
she threaded a strand of
yarn in and out, in and out,
in front of and then behind
the long lengths of yarn that hung taut
between bars at the ceiling and the floor.

"Very good, girls!" said Tía Dolores.
The sisters looked up to see their aunt
watching them from the doorway. "I am
so pleased to find you hard at work.
Bless you!"

"*Gracias*, Tía Dolores," said the
sisters. They smiled at their aunt. Josefina
smiled at Teresita, too, who was standing
behind Tía Dolores. Teresita was Tía
Dolores's servant. She was a wise and

kind Navajo woman who had taught
Josefina how to weave.

"I have good news," Tía Dolores said
cheerfully. "Teresita and I have counted
the sacks of wool in the storeroom, and
there's plenty. Teresita says we should be
able to make a good number of blankets."
A week ago, a terrible flash flood had
killed most of the family's sheep. The
rancho could not survive without sheep to
provide meat, and wool for weaving and
trading. The family was pinning its hopes
on Tía Dolores's idea of using wool
they had in the storeroom
to weave blankets, which
they'd sell or trade to
buy sheep to start a new

herd. "The *americanos* come to Santa Fe to trade in the summer," said Tía Dolores, "so that's when we must have our blankets finished."

"That's good news, too," said Francisca. "That means we have plenty of time as well as plenty of wool. Summer's far away."

Tía Dolores was still smiling, but she shook her head. "I am afraid the time will fly by," she said. "We won't have enough blankets unless we all weave as much as we can, as fast as we can."

"Forgive me, Tía Dolores," said Clara. She sounded anxious. "I'm afraid if I weave quickly, I'll make mistakes."

Tía Dolores spoke earnestly. "You'll

do fine, Clara, if you try," she said. "Look at Josefina. She didn't know how to weave at all. But she tried very hard and she learned from Teresita so that now she can help weave, too. And remember, it was Josefina's enthusiasm that encouraged your Papá to agree to our weaving business in the first place. The fact that we're doing it at all is thanks to Josefina."

Josefina cast her eyes down. She blushed at Tía Dolores's praise.

"I have great faith in all of you girls," said Tía Dolores. "You'll work as hard *every* week as you have this first week to make our weaving business a success, won't you?"

"We will, Tía Dolores," promised

Josefina cast her eyes down. She blushed at Tía Dolores's praise.

Ana, Francisca, and Clara.

Josefina promised, too. As usual, Tía Dolores made everything seem possible. She was so full of energy that some of it seemed to spill over and splash out onto everyone around her. But secretly, Josefina was a little worried. Weaving was difficult for her. Teresita had taught her well, and yet she still made so many mistakes that Teresita often had to tell her to take out a row and do it over again. Josefina wondered how much help she could truly be. Then she squared her shoulders and pushed her worries away. With all her heart, she was determined to keep her promise to Tía Dolores. She was sure her sisters meant their promises, too.

And they did. All four sisters wove conscientiously and without complaining—for the next few days, anyway.

Then one gray day, not quite two weeks after the flood, Josefina, Clara, and Francisca were in the weaving room before Ana, Teresita, or Tía Dolores had arrived. Josefina and Francisca were picking burrs out of clumps of wool, and Clara was trying to spin wool into yarn. Clara's hands were not quick. Again and again, the spindle bounced and skittered away from her.

"Oh!" Clara wailed. "I hate spinning. I don't like doing things fast. The spindle spins so fast that it makes me

dizzy. I feel like a spinning top."

"I feel like a shepherd," Francisca groused, "completely surrounded by wool. Soon I'll *look* like a shepherd, too, because even with all this weaving we're doing, we're not making anything pretty for ourselves to wear."

Josefina decided to try to cheer her sisters. She turned to Francisca and made a comically long face. In a low, sad voice, she sang an old song they all knew:

The life of the shepherd
is the saddest of all,
keeping up with the sheep,
only dressing up on Sundays . . .

Clara laughed. Francisca did, too, but her voice had a sting in it as she said,

"At least I'm not a sheep, Josefina, like you are." Francisca plunked her clump of wool on top of Josefina's head. "You're a baby sheep so eager to please that you follow wherever the shepherd—or in this case, shepherdess—leads."

"Little Josefina," teased Clara, "a little sheep. *Baa, baa, baa.*"

Josefina pretended to smile at her sisters' teasing. When she tried to brush the wool off her head, burrs caught in her hair. She had to pull at the wool, which hurt so badly that it made her eyes water. Her feelings were hurt, too. She was used to Francisca's sharp tongue, but it wasn't like Clara to join Francisca against her. And it wasn't fair. Did her sisters think

she liked sitting there hour after hour
weaving? Did they think she liked undo-
ing her mistakes, no matter how kindly
Teresita asked her to? Well, she did *not*.

✽

Cheerful sunshine slanted through
the open door of the weaving room and

made a bright, inviting path across the floor. Josefina swallowed a sigh. How she wished she could jump up and run out-side along that sunny path! But she knew she must not stop weaving, even though she'd been at it so long this morning that her legs, folded beneath her, had fallen asleep. Her arms were so tired that they seemed to want to go to sleep, too.

The weaving business was in its third week now, and things were not going well. Ana's baby son was ill, so Ana had not been able to weave for the past several

days. Tía Dolores and Teresita were so busy washing and dyeing wool that they were seldom in the weaving room, either. All this

morning, Josefina and Clara had had only
each other for company. They both looked
up from their looms when Francisca finally
sashayed into the room.

"Well, well," said Clara. "Here you
are at last."

Francisca yawned extravagantly in
answer. She sat at her loom and began
to weave, quickly, carelessly, and noisily.

"You'll make mistakes if you weave
so fast," Clara warned.

Francisca ignored her. If anything,
she began to weave faster.

Clara was annoyed. She looked away
from Francisca and her eyes fell on
Josefina's loom. She stopped weaving
and came over to study Josefina's work.

"You made a mistake, Josefina," she said, pointing. "Look. All of the rows you've done since your mistake will have to be taken out."

Josefina saw that Clara was right. Her heart sank. Two days' worth of weaving would have to be undone and then redone. "I hate having to fix my mistakes," she moaned.

"I'll do it," said Clara eagerly.

"No!" said Josefina. She was angry at herself and angry at Clara because Clara seemed just the tiniest bit pleased to have given her such bad news. Then Josefina saw something that made her angry at Francisca, too. "Francisca, what are you doing?" Josefina asked. "That's my red wool you're using. Stop!"

Francisca didn't stop. She shrugged. "Use my wool if you're in such a hurry," she said.

"But your red wool is knotty," said Josefina. "You dyed it red while it still had burrs in it."

"No one will notice a few burrs in your bumpy mess of a blanket," Francisca said coolly. "At least I . . ." But just then, Josefina snatched the red wool away from her. "Give it back," Francisca demanded. "Don't be so stingy. You're not using it."

"Not yet," replied Josefina, "but . . ."

"Not any time soon," Clara cut in. "You are the slowest weaver in the world, Josefina, even on that little loom."

"You're not very fast, either," said Josefina hotly.

"I'm slow but I'm steady," said Clara. "I don't make mistakes the way you and Francisca do."

"Your blankets are dull," Francisca said to Clara.

"Dull?" Clara repeated.

"*Sí,*" Francisca said. "Duller than the wool that's still on the sheep! I'm the only one who truly knows how to put the colors together." This was true. Josefina and Clara could not deny that Francisca's blankets were the most beautiful. Francisca added, "And I'm the fastest weaver, too."

16

"Because you're the most careless," Josefina said.

"When you bother to weave at all," said Clara, "which is hardly ever."

"You expect us to card your wool for you," said Josefina.

"I hate to card wool," said Francisca. "It's too slow."

"Well, I hate to spin wool," said Clara. "It's too fast."

"And I hate taking out mistakes and starting over," said Josefina.

At that, both Clara and Francisca whirled to face Josefina. "You should have thought of that before you got us into the weaving business," said Clara.

"Yes," said Francisca. "It's all your

fault. As Tía Dolores said, we're in this business thanks to *you*, Josefina!"

Josefina could stand no more. She jumped to her feet and stormed out, leaving her loom in a knotted, tangled mess. Her feelings were knotted and tangled, too, and her cheeks felt hot. She was sure that they were as red as the wool she had jammed into her pocket so that Francisca couldn't use it.

Josefina yanked the door to the weaving room shut behind her and ran to the little flower garden her mother had planted in a corner of the courtyard. She knelt down by the flowers and tried to calm herself. The flowers had been battered by the storm that caused the flood.

They leaned every which way, and some lay flat in the dirt. Josefina tried to straighten them and help them stand up, but they flopped down, defeated and disheartened, as soon as she took her hand away. Josefina swiped away a tear. She felt defeated and disheartened, too. She had never had such a terrible fight with her sisters before.

"Ah, Josefina!" said Teresita, coming toward her. "Here you are. I couldn't find you in the weaving room. I need your help. I'm going up into the hills to gather plants to make dyes. Your Tía Dolores says you know all the best places to look for plants. Will you come with me?"

Josefina could only nod.

"Good, then," said Teresita, handing Josefina a collecting basket like the one she carried. If she noticed Josefina's red, tear-streaked cheeks, she was too polite and kind to say anything about them.

As Teresita and Josefina climbed up the hill behind the orchard, a brisk, playful wind cooled Josefina's cheeks. Teresita walked quickly. Josefina, stretching her legs to keep up, felt the tight knot of anger inside her chest stretch and loosen, too. It was impossible to be downhearted under such a blue, blue sky decorated with high white clouds. It felt wonderful to Josefina to be outside, moving freely.

It felt wonderful to be helpful, too. Josefina knew where to find all the plants Teresita needed.

"Have you seen *cañaigre* growing on this hillside?" Teresita asked.

"Sí!" said Josefina. "Follow me!" She led Teresita to a sunny spot where cañaigre plants grew thick.

"We'll slice and dry these cañaigre roots to make gold and orange dyes,"

Teresita told Josefina as they put some roots in their baskets.

Josefina found *capulín* bushes for Teresita and helped her pick the berries, which Teresita said made dark pink dye. When Teresita asked for rabbit brush, Josefina led her to a hillside covered with it. "Rabbit brush blossoms make a lovely yellow dye," said Teresita.

"And Mamá told me the stems make green dye," Josefina said.

"That's right," said Teresita.

"I know where there are walnut trees, too," said Josefina eagerly. "Mamá taught me that walnut hulls make good dark brown and black dyes."

Teresita smiled. "I can see that I chose a very good helper," she said. "Lead the way, Josefina."

After they collected the walnuts, Josefina and Teresita walked back to the rancho. "I have such a funny collection of things in my basket," Josefina said, swinging her basket beside her. "Stems, roots, blossoms, berries, and nuts."

"Each one is important and necessary," said Teresita, "because each one makes a different color dye."

"These roots and berries are sort of like people," Josefina said. "Different ones are good at different things."

"Sí," agreed Teresita. "And we need the different abilities that people have,

*"These roots and berries are sort of like people," Josefina said.
"Different ones are good at different things."*

just as we need all the different colors,
to make our blankets beautiful."

Josefina was quiet, thinking about
what Teresita had said. It reminded her
of her sisters. Each sister was good at
what she *liked* to do and not so good at
what she did *not* like to do. Clara didn't
mind carding, but she hated to spin
because it was too fast. Francisca hated
to card because it was too slow, but she
was good at spinning and choosing colors. Josefina hated to undo her weaving
mistakes, but Clara liked taking out rows.
Maybe they could help one another.
Instead of each sister doing all the steps
in weaving, maybe each could do only
the step she liked best.

Josefina put her free hand in her pocket and pulled out her red wool. Would her idea work? she wondered. She grinned to herself. One thing was for sure—it could not make things worse. *It's worth a try*, she decided.

❉

Josefina was in front of her loom, carding wool, when Clara and Francisca came into the weaving room the next morning.

"What's this?" asked Francisca. She picked up a thick skein of beautiful, perfect red wool from the stool at her loom.

"Oh, I prepared that for you," said Josefina.

Francisca raised her eyebrows. "Gracias," she said. "But why?"

"Well," said Josefina, "in return, I'd like you to help Clara choose colors for her blanket. Will you?"

"Sí," said Francisca. "I'd like to, but . . ." She looked at Clara uncertainly.

Clara smiled. "I could use your help," she admitted.

"And Clara," said Josefina, "when you have time, could you help me?" She nodded at the tangled mess on her loom. "Will you take out these rows and help me fix the mistake I made?"

"I'd be glad to," said Clara. "That's work I like to do."

Francisca put her hands on her hips.

"What's going on here, Josefina?" she asked.

Josefina shrugged and grinned. "I just thought we could help one another," she said simply. "We'll all keep on weaving, of course, but we can share the other work. Each one of us can do the parts we like to do."

Francisca and Clara looked at each other and burst out laughing. "That's a wonderful idea, Josefina," Francisca said. "I'm good at doing things I like to do!"

"We all are," said Clara.

Josefina smiled. "I have another idea, too," she said. "Would you like to go on a picnic tomorrow? We can go up into the hills, and I will show you the plants that make the dyes. Teresita taught me some new ones."

"That would be fun!" said Francisca.

"Having fun is something we are all very good at, isn't it?" joked Josefina.

Her sisters certainly agreed. And, as the days went on, they also agreed that Josefina's idea about helping one another made weaving much more pleasant. The weaving business went smoothly—thanks to Josefina.

VALERIE TRIPP

At 9   Now

When I was in New Mexico, I learned how to make beautifully colored dyes from all sorts of things: leaves, stems, roots, berries, flowers—and even ground-up bugs. Just like Josefina, I loved finding out which things made which colors. For example, the bugs made a brilliant red!

Valerie Tripp has written forty-seven books in The American Girls Collection, including eleven about Josefina.

A PEEK INTO
THE PAST

Blankets woven by New Mexicans in
Josefina's time were as beautiful as the
land they came from. They were made of
the soft wool of the *churro* sheep
that were raised on the ranchos.
The wool was colored with rich
yellow, gold, and dark brown
dyes made from the plants and
trees that grew nearby. And the
blankets were brightened with
bits of red wool and bands of
indigo wool as blue as the
New Mexican sky.

*A New Mexican blanket
woven in the mid-1800s*

Each beautiful blanket required many hours of hard work. After men sheared the sheep, women and girls washed the wool and removed any burrs or twigs. Then they used brushes to *card*, or untangle, the wool. Next, they prepared dyes using roots, berries, blossoms, and nuts they had gathered.

Carding brushes had stiff bristles for untangling wool.

New Mexicans also used dyes imported from farther south in Mexico, such as indigo and cochineal. *Indigo* was a deep blue dye made from plants, which could be used

These dried insects were ground into powder to make cochineal.

alone or mixed with yellow dye to create green. *Cochineal* was a crimson red dye made from tiny insects. Each pound of cochineal required 70,000 insects, so the dye was very expensive. No wonder Josefina guarded her red wool closely!

Weavers spun the dyed wool into yarn and used it to create colorful patterns on their blankets. They wove stripes of blue, brown, yellow, and white wool, and perhaps a stripe or two of the cherished red wool. Some weavers added diamond, leaf, or zigzag designs borrowed from Saltillo *sarapes*, finely woven ponchos made in Saltillo and other towns in northern Mexico.

Navajo Indians wove blankets with designs similar to those woven into their baskets. They wove rows of triangles or the "Spider Woman's Cross," named after the mythical woman who taught the Navajo how to weave. Blankets woven by Indian servants in

A basket and dress showing the Spider Woman's Cross

New Mexican households came to be known as "servant blankets." They often showed a combination of Navajo and New Mexican designs.

One such blanket was woven by a Navajo servant named Rosario. Rosario had been taken captive by Spanish settlers and brought to live with a priest named Padre Martínez. Rosario missed her people, but the padre was kind to her, and she eventually made a new life with him. When, years later, he offered Rosario her freedom, she chose to stay with him. To thank him for his kindness, she wove him a sarape. She thought,

I'll make it a bit Navajo and the rest Spanish, for I am both now. I'll use white for the pureness, nobleness and sincerity of the padre, and I'll use black for the sorrow I . . . went

Rosario wove on a Navajo loom much like Teresita's.

through many years ago. And I'll put in red for the courage we all have to have.

Both Indians and New Mexicans wove blankets as thank-you gifts for personal favors. Blankets were also given to new brides as wedding gifts from the groom's family. These blankets were made of silky white wool and usually had a single brown stripe at the center. Small bits of colored yarn were added later to give new life to old blankets.

Most blankets, though, were made for use in the weaver's own household or for trade. New Mexicans wove thick wool sarapes to wear in the winter or to use as sleeping blankets at night. Weavers

The dashes of red and blue wool were added long after this wedding blanket was woven.

This Mexican man wears a colorful sarape.

made other blankets to use as rugs, saddle blankets, wall coverings, and padding on *bancos*, or benches.

Blankets were also woven to trade in Mexico City for necessities like iron tools and dry goods and for luxuries like chocolate and china. New Mexicans traded blankets to Indians in exchange for pottery, baskets, and buffalo hides. And when the Santa Fe Trail opened in 1821, New Mexicans began trading with Americans as well.

Trade with Americans would change weaving in many ways. Americans brought cotton cloth and ready-made clothing, which meant New Mexicans began weaving less clothing and more blankets for trade. In the 1860s, Americans introduced *aniline*, or artificial, dyes, and in the 1870s, machine-spun yarns. These dyes and yarns made weaving easier,

American traders also brought shoes, glass bottles, toys, mirrors, and tools.

but aniline dyes faded over time, so blankets didn't retain their beauty.

Today, some New Mexicans continue to weave blankets with real wool and natural dyes. In Chimayó, New Mexico, there are families who have been in business since the early 1700s. The traditional methods take time, but the finished blankets provide a valuable—and colorful—link to New Mexico's past.

DYE A T-SHIRT
Make a golden dye from onion skins!

People in Josefina's time couldn't buy packaged dyes from the grocery store the way we can today. They made most of their dyes from the flowers, berries, leaves, and roots of plants that grew near their homes.

You can make a natural dye using onion skins, which will give your T-shirt a deep golden glow. Tie rubber bands around the shirt before dyeing it to create rays of "sunshine"!

YOU WILL NEED:

♥ *An adult to help you*
Dry outer skins from 6 onions*
2-gallon stockpot
Slotted spoon
White, all-cotton T-shirt
6 rubber bands
2 tablespoons of white vinegar
Plastic garbage bag

*Ask the produce manager at your grocery store for the leftover skins in the onion bin.

1. Put the onion skins in the pot. Add water until the pot is a little more than halfway full.

2. Have an adult help you heat the water to a boil. Turn down the heat, and let the water simmer for 20 minutes. Let cool.

3. Use the slotted spoon to scoop out the onion skins. Throw the onion skins away.

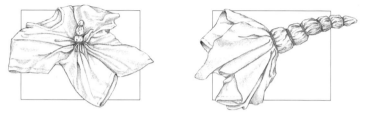

4. To create a tie-dyed look, hold the T-shirt from a point in the center. Twist a rubber band around that point. Add another rubber band an inch or so away from the first. Keep adding rubber bands until you've reached the end of the T-shirt.

5. Once again, have an adult help you heat the water in the pot to a boil. Turn off the heat, and immediately place the T-shirt into the water.

6. Add the vinegar to the water to set the dye. Let the shirt soak in the dye bath for 1 hour.

7. Fill a sink with cool water. Remove the T-shirt from the pot, wring it out, and place it in the sink to wash out remaining dye.

8. Remove the rubber bands, then wring out the shirt. Lay it flat on a garbage bag to dry.

9. Be careful when washing the shirt the first few times. Some of the dye may come out, so don't wash the shirt with other clothes!

GLOSSARY OF SPANISH WORDS

americanos *(ah-meh-ree-KAH-nohs)*—men from the United States

banco *(BAHN-koh)*—bench

cañaigre *(kah-NYAH-gray)*—a flowering plant that grows in the Southwest. Cañaigre roots are used to make gold, orange, and brown dyes.

capulín *(kah-poo-LEEN)*—or chokecherry. Berries were used for dyes as well as jam, jelly, and stomach medicine.

churro *(CHOO-ro)*—small, sturdy sheep

gracias *(GRAH-see-ahs)*—thank you

padre *(PAH-dreh)*—the title for a priest. It means "Father."

rancho *(RAHN-cho)*—a farm or ranch where crops are grown and animals are raised

Santa Fe *(SAHN-tah FEH)*—the capital city of New Mexico. Its name means "Holy Faith."

sarape *(sah-RAH-peh)*—a warm blanket that is wrapped around the shoulders or worn as a poncho.

sí *(SEE)*—yes

tía *(TEE-ah)*—aunt